Published in the UK by Scholastic Children's Books, 2019
Euston House, 24 Eversholt Street, London, NW1 1DB, UK
A division of Scholastic Limited.

London – New York – Toronto – Sydney – Auckland
Mexico City – New Delhi – Hong Kong

Text © Alice Hemming, 2019
Cover characters and inside Illustrations by Kerry LaRue © Scholastic Ltd,
2019

ISBN 978 1407 19668 8

A CIP catalogue record for this book is available from the British Library.

Printed by CPI Group (UK) Ltd, Croydon, CR0 4YY
Papers used by Scholastic Children's Books are made
from wood grown in sustainable forests.

1 3 5 7 9 10 8 6 4 2

www.scholastic.co.uk

for Lottie (and family)

Chapter 1

Camp BigToes

Rose's Mum gave her a goodbye hug.
"Have an *amazing* time at summer camp.
I'm sure you will!"

Rose wished that *she* could be as
confident. She had been on a school trip
before, but just for one night. Camp
would be *three whole nights* without
anyone she knew. Questions whirled

around her brain. *What would the food be like? Would she make any friends?* And the biggest question of all, *Would Wriggly be OK?* She gave her fluffy cockapoo one last cuddle, then waved goodbye as he trotted off on the lead with Mum and Dad. Tears pricked at Rose's eyes. Saying goodbye to Wriggly was hard. He probably thought he was going on a nice walk through the woods, but her parents were actually taking him to the kennels around the corner. They were going to a wedding and couldn't take him with them. Mum and Dad said that the kennels were like summer camp for dogs but Rose didn't like the thought of being away from him.

Rose shook the thought from her mind. It was a sunny day, she was here at summer camp and she was going to try to have fun. A person with a blue Camp Bickrose T-Shirt and a swingy high ponytail bounded over. "Hi, Rose, my name is Jess and I'm going to be your Group Leader here at Bickrose Hall. I'll show you the ropes and make sure you're in the right place at the right time."

Jess beckoned another girl over. "This is Oralie, she's one of your cabin mates. She got here early, so already knows where everything is. She'll show you to your room."

As soon as Rose saw Oralie she felt better. Oralie had bright pink round glasses and a big smile. Her black hair stuck out around her head in a beautiful frizz. She looked like a lot of fun.

"Hi," said Rose, smiling back shyly. As she followed Oralie to their cabin, Oralie talked all the way. "I got here early because my dad is working at the camp. He's only here until Wednesday, though, so at least I get one day all by myself. He has promised that I can pretend I don't know him the rest of the time!"

As Oralie talked, Rose looked around her, taking it all in. Bickrose Hall was a big mansion house set out in the countryside, surrounded by woodland.

"This is the girls' accommodation," said Oralie, pointing to the three log cabins to the right of the main building. "Each cabin has two rooms."

Oralie led them to the first cabin,

through the main door and then into the left-hand room. It was small and comfortable-looking with yellow walls and bright bedspreads. Sun streamed through the window, shining light on to the two bunk beds on each side of the room. There was a chest of drawers at the foot of each bed, and a storage box and metal locker on the wall for each girl.

Oralie spread out her arms in an excited welcome. "This is going to be our home for the next three nights! I haven't put my stuff on any of the beds yet," she continued, looking at the bunk beds. "I didn't know where people would want to sleep. Do you snore?"

"I don't think so," said Rose. Even if she did, how would she ever know?

"Great! Would you like to be my bunkmate, then?"

"I'd love to," Rose said, pleased that she'd made such a fun friend already.

"Top or bottom?" asked Oralie

"I don't mind," said Rose.

Oralie put her hands on her hips. "I really, *really* don't mind. You decide!"

"Then, I guess ... bottom?"

Rose unzipped her holdall and began putting her leggings and T-shirts into the drawers. Then the door opened and two more faces peeped in.

"Is this 1A?" asked the first girl, who had black shiny hair in a bob and a serious face. "I'm Yasmeen, by the way."

"... and I'm Amber," said the other girl, wearing a baseball cap with long black hair tucked underneath.

"Yes, this is 1A – are you our roommates?" asked Oralie.

They nodded. "Jess sent us here. She

said we have five minutes to unpack
before the camp tour begins."

While Amber and Yasmeen put their
things on the other bunk beds, they all
talked non-stop, trying to find out as
much as they could about each other
before the tour began. Rose knew she
was being quieter than usual, but she was
still feeling a little overwhelmed by it all.

They heard Jess bang on the door

of the room opposite before banging on their door too. "Time for the tour, everybody! This is your chance to find out where everything is. Ask me anything!"

Jess led their cabin around the grounds, telling them anything and everything they needed to know. The girls in 1B seemed nice enough, but were a couple of years older than everyone in Rose's cabin and stuck together in a giggling group.

There was so much to see at Camp Bickrose: art and music studios, a high ropes course, an archery centre, tennis courts, even an outdoor swimming pool. Amber's eyes lit up when she saw the pool. "Will we be going in there?"

"If it's hot enough," said Jess. Then, pointing to a dirt track outside the grounds, she said, "There's a farm over there. They have all sorts of animals, even llamas. Hence the llama trekking option on Sunday."

A murmur of excitement spread across the group. *Everyone* wanted to do the llama trekking!

Rose was starting to feel hot with her hoody on and unzipped it. There was something bulky in the pocket – what was it? Pulling it out, she saw: it was one of Wriggly's favourite dog chews, left over from her last walk with him at home. That was only this morning, but somehow it felt like for ever ago. As she tied her hoody around her waist she wondered if she was going to be OK here at Camp Bickrose, however lovely people seemed to be.

After they had toured the grounds, they got to go inside Bickrose Hall itself.

There was a big dining hall where they would eat all their meals, a TV room with big comfy chairs and sofas, and a games room with table tennis and pool tables. "And that's the camp shop," said Jess, waving in the direction of a small shop stocked with sweets, chocolates, souvenirs and gifts.

"Your parents have given me your pocket money, and I'll be handing it out in *small amounts* so that you can't spend it all on chocolate!" said Jess. "I highly recommend the squishy banana sweets, though."

When the tour was over, everyone gathered outside the hall. A CAMP BICKROSE banner was pinned above the door, with boards standing below that displayed the timetable for the next few days. Oralie gazed up at the banner, knitting her eyebrows together. "Camp Bickrose? I never knew it was called that," she said.

"Of course it is — Camp Bickrose, after Bickrose Hall!" said Yasmeen.

"What did you think it was called?" asked Rose.

Oralie put her face in her hands and mumbled, "You're going to think I'm really silly. . ."

"Go on, tell us," cajoled Amber.

Oralie looked up. "I thought it was Camp BigToes! I never saw it written down!"

Everyone laughed. Rose giggled until her stomach hurt. What had she been worrying about? She was going to love it here at Camp BigToes. She just had to stop thinking about Wriggly.

Chapter 2

The Treasure Box

Jess sent them back to their cabins with
piles of paper, card and colouring pens,
and a challenge: before dinner, they had
to come up with a name for their room
and decorate a sign for the door.

"The most beautifully decorated and —
not forgetting — *tidiest* room will win a
prize. Be as creative as you like. We'll be

doing room inspections every day, and you can gain points for tidiness. And at the end of the weekend we'll judge the winners!"

Rose sat on the floor between the bunk beds. "Shall I make our room sign? I love art."

"Me too," said Yasmeen. "And I can do good bubble writing. Shall I draw out nameplates to go above each of our beds?"

"That would be great," said Oralie. "I'm rubbish at drawing but I can cut things out."

Amber picked up a pair of scissors. "I'll help."

Yasmeen started writing their names straight away but Rose stared at her sheet of card. "What's our room name going to be?"

There was silence. Everyone looked at one another with blank faces. "What have 1B called themselves?" asked Oralie.

Amber opened the door and took a peek at their sign. It read BICKROSE BESTIES.

"I'm sure we can think of something more original. We could use our initials as a starting point," said Yasmeen.

Amber got out a pen and notepad and began scribbling.

"Maybe our initials spell out a word. O–A–R–Y? Y–O–R–A? O–R–A–Y?"

"ORAY. Like 'Ip, 'Ip, 'Oray?" said Oralie.

Rose looked doubtful. "I'm not so sure. . ."

"What about if we use our surnames too?" suggested Amber. "I'm Amber Beau – AB." She wrote it down.

"I'm Rose Gold, like the metal," said Rose.

Yasmeen laughed. "I'm Yasmeen Silver! Maybe that's why they put us in the same room."

"You both have shiny surnames!" said Oralie. "Ooh – hang on – Amber is a shiny name too. Isn't Amber a gemstone?"

Amber nodded. "I think it means 'sky' in Hindi but it's a gemstone as well. It's actually fossilised tree resin but you do get it made into necklaces and bracelets and stuff."

Oralie laughed. "We could be the shiny happy people. Or something to do with treasure! The Treasure Chest? Or the Treasure Box?"

"I like 'Treasure Box'," agreed Rose, writing it lightly in capitals on the blank

page. She sketched the outline of an open treasure chest beneath it.

"But what about Oralie?" asked Yasmeen, who didn't want to leave anyone out. "Is your name shiny?"

"No, my surname is Sands, so not at all shiny. I want a shiny name!" she laughed. "I don't mind really. Maybe our treasure box could be buried in the sand?"

"Good idea! A pirate theme," said Yasmeen.

Amber picked up a pile of shiny metallic card. "I'll cut our names out from different coloured card. Pink for Rose, silver for Yasmeen, orange for Amber and gold for Oralie."

All of a sudden, the ideas came thick and fast.

"I'll use this brown corrugated card to cover the storage box under the window. We can make it look like a treasure chest," said Oralie.

"That's such a good idea! And we need treasure inside. I wonder if the camp shop sells chocolate coins. . ."

"Let's look tomorrow."

"We could make a map for the door!"

"And turn our bunk bed post into a palm tree!"

Rose was so happy drawing and creating with her new friends that for a whole hour she didn't think once about being homesick.

Chapter 3

Yapping Like a Sea Lion

There wasn't a moment to sit still at camp! After the decorating, it was time for dinner. Rose needn't have worried about the food – it was lovely. They got to choose from about three different options and help themselves to any extras they fancied from the salad bar. Rose had a huge portion of lasagne and then chocolate mousse for pudding.

Then came the Opening Campfire. Everyone made their way to a special area around the back of the hall. They sat on wooden seats in a semicircle while Oralie's dad, Mr Sands, got a blazing fire going in the middle. Jess and the others taught them songs and told stories. Jess said they would all be best friends by the end of the week. Rose looked at her three roommates, sitting beside her. She hoped so.

Afterwards, they chatted into the evening until Jess knocked on their door and said, "Lights out now, you've got an early start in the morning."

Eventually, everyone went quiet. So quiet that Rose could hear her roommates shifting and sighing in their beds. Oralie breathed heavily. Was she asleep already? Rose wished she could sleep. In the silence and the dark, Rose's homesickness grew bigger than it had been outside in the sunshine. Light filtered through the cracks in the blind, making a triangle on the ceiling. Rose stared at the pattern, feeling more awake than ever.

In the bottom bunk opposite, Amber shuffled up to a sitting position. "Can't you sleep?" she whispered.

"No," said Rose quietly.

"Are you homesick?" Amber asked. "This is my third time at summer camp. The first time I was a bit sad, but now I know how much fun it's going to be."

Yasmeen climbed down from the bunk above and sat next to Amber. "Do you miss your mum and dad?"

Rose rolled on to her side. "I do miss them, but it's my dog I miss the most. He's like my best friend and my teddy bear all

rolled into one. He's a bundle of mischief."

Amber and Yasmeen made sympathetic noises and Rose carried on. "At home, he sleeps on my bed every night. He was never supposed to, but Mum and Dad gave up in the end. And tonight he's in kennels, miles away from me. How is Wriggly going to sleep?"

"Wriggly is a funny name!" said a voice from the bunk above. Oralie wasn't asleep after all.

"That's nothing. My dog's called Fluffikins!" said Amber.

"FLUFFIKINS?" said Oralie, forgetting to whisper.

"Yes, my parents let my little sister pick the name when we got her. She was only three."

Yasmeen laughed. "My dog, Mabel, is an old girl now so she's not very fluffy or much of a wriggler, but she loves cuddles. I rest my feet on her when they get cold. I miss Mabel, too."

Oralie leaned over the side of her bed and looked down at Rose. "Noooooo! Not only do you all have shiny names, you all have dogs except me! I have wanted a dog FOR EVER. I keep asking my dad."

"What does he say?" asked Yasmeen.

"He says things like, 'never say never' and 'maybe when you're old enough to take a dog for walks'."

"That's better than a 'no'. Anyway, you are still part of the Treasure Box, even without a shiny name or a dog," said Rose. She was starting to feel a bit better after sharing her feelings with her new friends.

Oralie jumped to her feet and grabbed the bunk bed ladder. "Thanks. Hey,

Rose, I'm coming down!"

Rose shifted over to make room by her pillow but Oralie climbed past her and down to the bottom of the bed. "What are you doing?" asked Rose, with a laugh.

"I'm going to lie on your feet like Wriggly does until you feel better."

Rose laughed. "If you're really going to be like Wriggly then you need to do a little yappy sound, a bit like a sea lion.

Oralie yapped. "What, like this?"

"No, more like this," said Rose, yapping higher.

Amber and Yasmeen laughed and joined in with the dog impressions. Then, behind all the noise, Rose thought she heard an echo from outside, like a real dog. She sat bolt upright. "Shhhh, everyone. Listen!"

They listened. There was a definite barking sound.

"It's a dog! Our impressions must have summoned it. There are probably *hundreds* of dogs surrounding the cabin by now," said Yasmeen,

Everyone giggled but Rose kept listening intently. "It's Wriggly. He's outside! I'd recognize that yap anywhere."

Oralie shook her head sadly. "Rose has finally lost it, girls. . ."

The other two laughed.

Rose climbed out of bed and put on her dressing gown. "I'm going outside."

"In your *pyjamas*?" said Yasmeen, but Rose was already at the door.

"Wait! I'll come too. And we'll need a torch," said Amber, grabbing one from her bedside locker and following Rose.

"We'll stay here – you'll need

someone to let you back in," said Oralie, remembering that the internal doors opened from the inside but not the outside. Not unless you had a key.

The two girls crept slowly out of the cabin. It was fully dark now, darker than at home. Rose shivered and pulled her dressing gown tighter around herself.

They walked around the side of the cabin, Amber flashing the beam of torchlight to the right and left. The light shone on a bundle of cream fur. A bundle of fur that was racing towards them at super-speed. A bundle of fur that leaped into Rose's arms and licked her face all over.

"Wriggly?" said Rose.

"It can't be!" said Amber.

But it was.

Chapter 4

Just Until Morning

Oralie's and Yameen's jaws nearly hit the bottom bunks when Rose walked in with Wriggly in her arms.

"How did he *get* here?" asked Oralie, when she had found her voice.

Rose shook her head from side to side. "He must have escaped from the kennels and come all the way here! Clever boy!"

Rose put Wriggly on the floor and he raced around the room, making the girls laugh. Then he jumped on to Rose's bed. Oralie gave him a good stroke, and he loved the attention.

"He must be hungry after his journey here. Have we got anything to feed him?" asked Amber.

Rose remembered the treat that she'd found in her pocket earlier. "I've got a dog biscuit. And a banana!"

Oralie raised an eyebrow. "Dogs can eat bananas?"

"Wriggly loves bananas," said Rose, unpeeling it and handing it to him in bite-sized chunks. He gobbled each one up hungrily.

"We have to tell someone. Let's get the night leader," said Yasmeen.

Rose's face fell. "But they'll take him straight home. Can't he stay just until the morning?"

Wriggly yawned. Rose cuddled him and he rested his chin on her knees. "Look, he's really tired. If I know Wriggly, he'll fall asleep straight away. I'll tell Jess that he turned up in the middle of the night and I didn't want to wake anyone."

They all agreed and got back into their beds, where Wriggly adopted his favourite position, lying across Rose's feet. With Wriggly there, Rose's homesickness drifted away and she fell asleep smiling.

Chapter 5

Early Morning Energizer

The girls were all up *way* before the
seven-thirty a.m. wake-up call. Rose
smuggled out Wriggly under her
dressing gown so that he could do his
business.

"Are you going to tell Jess about
Wriggly this morning?" asked Amber
when Rose brought him back inside.

Rose cuddled Wriggly tight and shrugged.

"We can't keep him here," said Yasmeen.

"But I can't send him back to the kennels," said Rose.

"What about your mum and dad? The kennels will call them and they'll be worried."

"We're allowed to make one phone call. I'll say that he's turned up here and camp have let him stay."

Yasmeen looked down at Wriggly. "What's he going to eat?" she said. "You can't feed him bananas all week!"

Wriggly barked and they all laughed.

"Let's pocket some extra sausages at breakfast!" said Oralie. "There's such a sausage mountain that no one will ever notice."

"We're not supposed to give him sausages. It can upset his tummy," said Rose. "Even though he loves them."

"NO WAY! You are telling me that dogs eat bananas but not sausages? Everything I thought I knew is a lie!" said Oralie dramatically.

Amber laughed. "OK, I have a plan. I'm going out on an early morning energizer. We'll stop in the village and I can go to the shop then."

"What in the name of BigToes is an early morning energizer?" asked Oralie.

"A morning run. For half an hour before breakfast."

"Who wants to go running when you could be tucking into the BigToes sausage mountain?"

Amber laughed. "We'll run through the village and I can go into the little shop. I'll take my rucksack so that people don't see the dog food."

"Are we really going to do this? What if we get caught?" said Yasmeen.

There was a knock at the door. Was it Jess? They all looked around, panicking.

"Just a minute!" called Amber.

Rose took Wriggly to the window and wrestled the latch open. The window didn't open all the way but it was big enough.

"It's the girls from 1B. Can you open up, please?" came the voice from behind the door.

Rose held Wriggly up to the gap and, luckily, he took the hint and jumped out as Amber opened the door.

Two of the Bickrose Besties came into the room. They were smiling but looking around as if they were searching

for something. They obviously knew
something was up. Rose hoped they
hadn't guessed exactly what.

Oralie stood in front of the window,
and Rose sat on the bed so that she
could still see out of the window.

"This is going to sound really odd,"

said the taller girl, "but we thought we heard *barking* coming from this room."

Oralie laughed so loudly that she made the girl jump. "Hahaha! Barking? Why would there be barking? It's not like we're hiding a dog in here or anything. Hahahaha!"

Rose tensed up. Wriggly was jumping up and down outside their window, his little teddy bear face and paws appearing every few seconds. He must have thought it was a game, but if the girls from 1B saw him… They were still standing at the door, looking around the room with their eyes narrowed.

"It was me!" cried Yasmeen suddenly. "I have a bad cough and it sounds like a bark. It's *really* embarrassing." The girls looked surprise as she began to cough a barking cough, covering her mouth with her hand, but the lie seemed to work.

"Er, OK... I hope you feel better soon," said the smaller one.

"Yeah ... see you at the team-building activity later," said the taller one, and they left.

When the door slammed shut, Oralie leaned back against it. "Phew, that was a close one! You're a brilliant actor, Yasmeen."

Yasmeen laughed. "I never knew that until just now!"

Rose opened the window again and called Wriggly to jump back inside.

He ran up to each of the girls in turn.

"He *is* super-cute," said Amber.

"It wasn't *that* hard to hide him after all," said Oralie.

Rose held out Wriggly, who did his

best big puppy eyes at them all.

"Does that mean he can stay for the rest of the camp?"

Amber and Oralie nodded. Yasmeen looked unsure.

"Yasmeen?" pleaded Rose.

"How can I refuse those big eyes?" said Yasmeen. "OK. I can't believe I'm saying yes, but OK."

"Then we all agree. Wriggly is the new member of room 1A," said Amber.

Chapter 6

Team Building

Amber's dog food plan worked brilliantly, and she was clever enough to buy pouches, not cans, so they didn't even need a tin opener.

Wriggly had to stay on his own in the cabin while they went to the first activity, which was called "Team Building" on the timetable. Rose felt a bit bad about it and left him a cardboard box and some socks to play with. "It's just for an hour or two," she said to him softly. "I'll check back on you at lunchtime."

The team-building activity was an obstacle course, which they would complete in their room groups. Jess showed them the route. It looked pretty easy. Just a wiggly walkway with a bridge, a crawl tunnel on the floor and some hanging tyres to climb through. There was a rope at waist level all the way along the course.

"But the twist is ... you will be wearing blindfolds the whole time."

"Oralie, you can lead the way," said Jess, tying on the first blindfold.

"This is going to be impossible!" said Oralie.

Jess tied on all the other blindfolds. "You'll be fine – just follow the rope with your hands and you won't lose your way."

Rose found it strange standing there in the dark with the sun on her back, but with Oralie up ahead, and Yasmeen's reassuring hand behind her, she knew she could do it.

Oralie was a good leader, shouting out directions to warn them what was coming up. Jess tried to put them off by tickling them with peacock feathers and throwing sponge balls at them, but they still managed to complete it in record time.

"You make such a good team," said Jess in awe, taking off all the blindfolds.

"We really do!" said Rose, grinning. She couldn't stop grinning since Wriggly had turned up and now she was really enjoying camp life.

Next they split up to do different activities. Rose and Yasmeen were in the art studio, painting plates. Rose painted a smiling cockapoo's face in the middle of her plate, surrounded by hearts all around the edges. Yasmeen split hers into segments and coloured each one a different colour of the rainbow.

Yasmeen was one of the quietest in their group and it was nice to spend a bit of time getting to know her. Yasmeen told Rose about her dog, Mabel, and about her friends at school. Rose told Yasmeen how she was entering an art competition in a magazine. The best thing was that they didn't have to talk the whole time and spent some of the session painting in happy silence. At the end of the session, they left the plates to go in the kiln; they would be able to collect them at the end of the week.

As they left the art studio, Yasmeen said, "I wonder how Amber and Oralie got on with the high ropes course." They didn't have to wait long to find out, as ten seconds later Oralie skipped towards them, shouting, "I'VE GOT A SHINY NAME TOO!"

Amber was smiling behind her.

Oralie took a big breath. "After the high ropes I was speaking to my dad about names and he said that Oralie means 'golden' in French because Mum's French, which means that I'm golden like you,

Rose, only you are *rose* gold and I am *yellow* gold like sand." The words came out so quickly, it was as if Oralie didn't take a breath the whole time.

"What did she just say?" said Yasmeen with a laugh.

"I *think* she said that her name means golden," said Rose.

"So we are *all* official *shiny* members of the Treasure Box?" said Amber.

Oralie nodded delightedly.

The four girls linked arms as they walked back to the cabin to check on Wriggly.

Unfortunately, Wriggly had chewed the cardboard box and swapped all their teddies on to the wrong beds. "At least he hasn't chewed up Bill Whiskers," said Oralie, inspecting her well-loved soft cat.

Suddenly they heard a voice outside the door.

"Inspection time!"

"Aaargh — it's Jess!" shrieked Amber, peering out of the door. "It looks like she's checking 1B first. What do we do with Wriggly?"

"Hide him, quick!" Oralie threw her blanket over Wriggly, which only got him excited because he thought it was another game. He started to bark.

"Out of the window, Wriggly, now!" said Rose, and he jumped outside like last time, but this time he carried on barking.

Rose looked around at the others in a panic. What were they going to do?

"Do something to hide the sound!" said Yasmeen.

Amber had a radio, which she turned

up to top volume. Oralie began singing along at the top of her voice and Yasmeen started bark-coughing again like she had before.

Rose ran frantically around, trying to hide any doggy evidence.

When Jess arrived, she put her hands over her ears.

"Wow, girls, you are a tidy and creative room — I love the name, by the way — but you are also the *noisiest* room I've seen yet. Can you turn that down a bit?"

Amber cautiously turned the music down a notch. What if Jess heard Wriggly now? But so far so good. Except, Rose had just realized that the empty packets of dog food were sticking out of the bin a bit. She crumpled up a sheet of paper and threw it to Yasmeen.

"Bin!" she shouted, making Jess raise an eyebrow. "Just saw a magazine lying on the floor. Can't have that. Way too messy," explained Rose.

Jess stood there for a moment, looking over the room again. After a while she sighed. "Well, I'm going to give you some points for tidiness but I know you're up to something – I just need to figure out what," she said. With a shrug and a smile, she left them to it.

Rose pulled Wriggly back into the cabin and the girls all fell on to her bed in a relieved heap.

"Phew, that was close," said Amber. "Wriggly is getting more wriggly by the minute."

"I think he's bored. I'll have to think of some way to take him out soon."

As luck would have it, the perfect excuse presented itself after lunch, when one of the group leaders stood up in the dining hall and made an announcement.

"I know swimming is on the timetable for this afternoon, but we are hoping that one room group will volunteer to collect firewood in the woods instead. We would be forever grateful, and you would earn ten points for your room."

Rose shot up her hand, crying, "We'll do it!" while the other girls nodded their agreement. The group leader looked at them in confusion – no one had ever been this excited about collecting firewood before, especially when it meant missing out on swimming.

"OK, then... Meet Mr Sands outside the cabin at three o'clock and he'll tell you what to do," they said.

Jess wandered over to their table with a knowing look on her face. "You girls seem very keen to miss swimming this afternoon. What are you up to?"

The girls looked at their plates.

"This doesn't, by any chance, have something to do with winning the cabin competition, does it?"

"Err, maybe?" said Amber

"Go on, then – enjoy your afternoon off, but don't get up to mischief!"

Chapter 7

Kindling

Mr Sands was tall and had a smile just like Oralie's.

"Thank you for volunteering to help, girls," he said kindly, when they met him outside the cabin. "We have plenty of big logs for the fire tonight but we are going to need to collect a lot of kindling. We need little twigs and sticks — but make sure they're dry."

Oralie grinned up at him as he handed each of them a basket. "No offence, Dad, but you're not coming too, are you? You did promise that I could pretend you weren't here!"

Oralie's dad laughed. "Yes, OK, but stay in this area behind the cabins. And I want you to *completely* fill up all those baskets. Otherwise there will be no campfire tonight. I'll be in the hall if you need me."

Mr Sands walked off and the girls all giggled.

"Well done, Oralie," said Amber. "The perfect excuse to walk Wriggly!"

Rose ran into the cabin to get him, while the others started filling their baskets. The grounds were full of sticks, so it didn't take long at all for the girls to collect loads of nice, dry kindling. Wriggly enjoyed himself too, barking at squirrels and trying to carry a stick that was twice as long as he was!

"I'm not sure that's completely helpful, Wriggly," said Rose.

Oralie held Wriggly's furry face between her hands and he dropped the stick. "I hope you realize we're missing swimming because of this?" she said. Wriggly jumped up and licked her cheek in reply.

"What time is it?" asked Yasmeen.

After collecting so much kindling, she was starting to feel a bit tired.

Oralie sat down abruptly on a fallen tree trunk. "I think it's ... picnic time! We don't have to take the wood back up to my dad for another half an hour, so I reckon we should have a snack. I've brought supplies!" She reached into her rucksack and pulled out four bags of crisps. The girls took them gratefully, but Amber grimaced when she looked at her packet. "Tomato ketchup flavour?"

Oralie nodded enthusiastically. "They sell them for fifty pence at the camp shop. I have eight pounds of pocket money to spend at camp, so that's four packets of crisps a day."

"What about your family? Don't you want to take them a present home?" asked Yasmeen.

"My dad's here already so he doesn't need a souvenir. I guess I could take something for my mum and my brother... I wonder if *they* like tomato ketchup crisps?"

The girls all laughed – Rose more than anyone. With Wriggly bounding about at her feet, she felt very glad she'd come to Camp BigToes.

Chapter 8

Campfire Chaos

Their kindling must have done the trick because the campfire that night seemed to blaze even bigger and brighter than it had done on Monday.

The whole camp sat around in a semicircle, their faces glowing in the firelight. Rose sat between Oralie and Yasmeen, and Amber sat to Oralie's left.

The leaders stood in the middle, in front of the fire, and got them all singing together. Some were songs that Rose knew from school and others were brand new. There was one about a penguin, where they had to join in with the actions, flapping their arms and legs. Then Jess taught them a new song:

Make new friends,
but keep the old.
One is silver,
the other gold.

They sang it all together, then in the round, with half the camp singing it first and the other half joining in after the first line. Yasmeen leaned in towards Rose and whispered, "I know this one. We learnt it at Brownies. There was another verse as well but I can't remember that."

After the singing, the leaders toasted marshmallows, squished them between two biscuits and passed them around. They munched and chatted on the wooden seats. Rose was sure that Wriggly would want to sleep after his long walk but they didn't want to risk him trashing the cabin, so they came up with lots of excuses to check on him.

"Jess, I've left my torch behind. Can I go back to the cabin to get it?" asked Amber.

"Of course — but take a friend with you."

Amber and Yasmeen reported back that Wriggly was fine.

"Jess, can I go to the toilet?" asked Yasmeen, twenty minutes later.

"Sure — go in pairs, please."

Yasmeen and Oralie reported back that Wriggly was still asleep.

"Jess, I'm freezing. Can I pop back to the cabin and grab my bobble hat?" asked Oralie, twenty minutes later.

"A bobble hat? In August?"

"I mean a thicker fleece," said Oralie.

"And me?" said Rose and Amber and Yasmeen.

"What are you girls up to?" asked Jess. This time all the girls ran back to the cabin together, giggling. Wriggly was awake and delighted to see them all.

"I think Jess is getting suspicious," said Yasmeen.

"Yes, but she thinks we're working on our room design," said Oralie.

"Anyway, the campfire will be over in half an hour and then we won't have to check on him any more," said Rose.

"What are we going to do with him tomorrow?" asked Yasmeen.

But Rose didn't have the chance to answer, because the door swung open, and standing there, arms folded, looking most unimpressed, was Jess.

Chapter 9

Found Out

Jess closed the door behind her. "Well? Can anybody tell me why there is a dog in your room?"

There was silence. Everyone looked at their feet. Rose picked up Wriggly for a cuddle.

Jess tried again. "Whose dog is it?"

"He's mine. He's called Wriggly," said Rose quietly.

"What? You didn't bring him with you, did you?"

"No, he found his way here all by himself from the kennels where he was staying." *Clever boy,* thought Rose, but she didn't say that aloud.

"And how long have you been keeping him here?"

The girls looked sideways at one another. But Rose thought that, since they had been found out, honesty was the best policy. "Since last night," she said.

"*Last night?* I *knew* you were up to something!"

Jess sat down on Yasmeen's bed. Rose held Wriggly on her lap and sent him telepathic instructions. *Look cute!* And he did. He fixed his big puppy dog eyes right on Jess.

Jess smiled. "He *is* very cute. But I *have* to tell the camp boss – I won't say that you've been hiding him all day," she said quickly, seeing fear in the girls' faces. "How about I tell the camp boss that he has just arrived? Maybe he took a long route from the kennels."

"Thank you, thank you, thank you!" cried the girls. Jess really was lovely.

"But you do know that he can't stay here any more, don't you?" she said to Rose gently.

Rose felt the tears welling up in her eyes. "Please don't make him go back to the kennels. I can't bear to think of him sleeping in a cage without me."

"I'm sorry, Rose, but we can't keep him here," said Jess. "We have strict health and safety rules. And it isn't fair on Wriggly."

Amber put her arms around Rose. "Don't cry. You'll get to see him in just two more days."

Rose burst into tears. Two days sounded like a really long time.

Oralie jumped up. "I've got an idea! Can I speak to my dad?"

Chapter 10

Llamas

Oralie dragged her dad back to their cabin and scooped Wriggly out of Rose's arms.

"Look at this little guy, Dad. How could you resist?" she said, pushing Wriggly into her dad's arms.

Mr Sands shifted Wriggly gently, and Wriggly wriggled in to get comfy. Mr

Sands smiled. "Just until Monday you say?"

Oralie's Dad and Jess made a few phone calls, including to the kennels and to Rose's mum and dad, who were very surprised to hear that Wriggly had been staying at the camp in secret. Jess explained how homesick Rose had felt and they weren't cross. It was soon all agreed: Oralie's dad would take Wriggly home and bring him back on Monday.

Wriggly seemed so happy to be with Mr Sands, and Rose just knew that they were going to look after Wriggly really well at Oralie's house. Before they went to bed, Oralie's dad sent pictures to Jess, for her to share with Rose. One was a selfie that he took with Wriggly at a stop-off on the journey home, one was

Wriggly investigating their garden, and then there was one of Wriggly in an impromptu dog box bed, chewing on a brand-new doggy toy.

"He looks so happy!" said Rose.

"So does my dad," said Oralie. "Maybe Wriggly will persuade him that we need a dog!"

Seeing that Wriggly was happy made Rose happy too, and now that they didn't have a big secret to keep, she felt the cloud of worry lift from her shoulders. The other girls felt happier too — they hadn't even realized how on edge they'd been feeling while they were worried about being caught.

Now they could all concentrate on the most important thing: having fun. That night, the girls slept more soundly than ever before.

The next day was Sunday and because it was their last full day at camp there were heaps of fun activities to get involved with.

First was the llama trek. A large group of them gathered together in front the hall, and everyone wore shorts or playsuits because the sun was high in the sky and it was hot. Everyone apart from Oralie, who wore baggy navy-blue waterproof trousers. "Why have you got those on?" said Jess, giving Oralie a strange look. "It's going to be thirty degrees today!"

Oralie looked down at her legs. "I've got my jogging bottoms on under these as well. I was worried that the llamas might be a bit uncomfortable. They've got kind of bumpy backs."

Jess laughed. "You don't *ride* the

llamas, Oralie. You lead them along. Go on, you've still got five minutes to get changed."

Everyone laughed good-heartedly as Oralie ran back to the cabin.

It turned out that they would walk their llamas on leads through the countryside. The llamas were gentle, curious creatures, and although they didn't carry the girls, they did carry their water bottles and

packed lunches. Rose's llama was called Martin and he had the longest eyelashes she had ever seen.

As they walked through the beautiful countryside, they sang all the songs they could remember from last night's campfire.

"I think this is my favourite place *ever*," said Oralie.

Rose smiled at her three new best friends. She had to agree. Amber was striding off ahead at the front of the group but she stopped and turned round.

"I've thought of some new words to that 'make new friends' song:

Brand new friends,
At Camp Bigtoes
Amber, Silver,
Gold and Rose."

"I love it! Just right for our Treasure Box group," said Rose.

"I wish I could remember the second verse," said Yasmeen.

Chapter 11

BigToes Boogie

That afternoon, the timetable read
"Bickrose Quiz" but Jess wandered
into the lunch hall with some giant
inflatables. "Because it's such a sunny
day, we thought we'd go swimming
again!" she called, and everyone cheered.

"Yay! We missed it yesterday because
of that pesky dog of yours!" said Oralie.

They got changed at top speed and rushed to the outdoor pool. They were so quick, they were the first ones there.

Jess threw in a giant inflatable llama pool toy and Oralie grabbed it straight away. She climbed in and lay back with her sunglasses on.

"This is the life! I did get to ride a llama after all!"

Amber swam under the water and tipped Oralie out of

the llama,
and then they
all took turns
relaxing on
the inflatable.
When it was
another group's
turn to have the
toy, they practised
handstands in the shallow end and swam
like sharks with their hands held above
their heads.

The sun
stayed high in
the sky and the
water sparkled
and Rose wished
they had another
week left at camp.

*

That night was the AuRevoir Disco in the main hall. The room was dark with brightly coloured disco lights and loud music. There were tables along one side with crisps and jugs of squash. Everyone dressed up and Jess gave them all deely boppers to wear. It was super hot but that didn't put anyone off dancing, and there was even a competition where each room had to create their own dance. Room 1B won and taught the whole camp their routine – "The Bickrose Besties Bickrose Boogie".

"BigToes Boogie sounds better," whispered Oralie through the clapping.

Then there was a mini awards ceremony and prizes were handed out for the bravest moment, best eater and all sorts of other things. The *Treasure Box* girls won the prize for the best room decoration. Their prize was a shiny two pound coin each to spend in the camp shop!

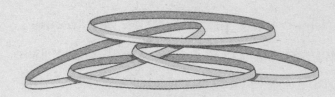

Chapter 12

A Circle Has No End

On the last morning, they went to the camp shop to spend their prize money.

Oralie held up some tomato ketchup crisps. "I could get four packets of these."

But Amber shook her head. "No, it needs to be something special that we can take home to remember our time here."

They looked through the rubbers and pens and paperweights, but nothing seemed quite right.

Then Yasmeen shrieked from over by the till. "I've found the perfect, PERFECT thing. Look."

She held up a bracelet. It was made of four narrower bracelets in different shiny metals joined together. There were two types of gold – one yellow and one rose – along with one silver and one orange. "I don't think it's real gold and silver. But still."

"NOOOOO WAY. That is amazingly perfect. It's like the four of us joined together in a bracelet," said Oralie. "But it looks expensive. I bet it's more than our prize money."

"It's £5.99," she said, "too much for each one of us to buy one, but what if we pooled together our prize money?" suggested Yasmeen.

She examined the bracelet closely. "There's just one piece of metal holding the four bracelets together. We could take that off and have one bracelet each. What do you think?"

There were smiles and nods of agreement all round.

"That means we'll have two whole pounds left over," said Amber, "and I think I know someone else who deserves a present."

"Wriggly?" said Oralie.

"Not Wriggly – he will be getting spoiled at your house! No, who has looked after us all week and made sure we didn't get into trouble for hiding Wriggly?"

"Jess!" they all cried. So they bought

the bracelet for themselves and some squishy banana sweets for Jess to say thank you.

Later, when they were waiting for their parents to arrive, Rose examined the rose gold bracelet on her arm. "This bracelet is lovely, but I think I've found the real treasure right here with all of you. I was homesick to begin with but I'm going to be *camp*sick when I leave you!"

Yasmeen sat down next to her. "We'll all stay in touch, won't we?"

Oralie and Amber joined them.

"Yes, definitely. But when will we see each other again? Next summer is a whole *year* away. We can't wait until then," said Oralie.

"Let's all ask our parents if we can

meet up. I bet you could stay at mine," said Amber.

"Give me your hands, everyone," said Yasmeen suddenly. They stood in a circle, crossed their arms and held each other's hands.

"I've finally remembered the second verse to that rhyme I told you!" she said.

"A circle is round,
It has no end.
That's how long,
I will be your friend."

"That is perfect," said Rose. "Best friends for ever!"

And their four shiny bracelets glinted in the sunshine.

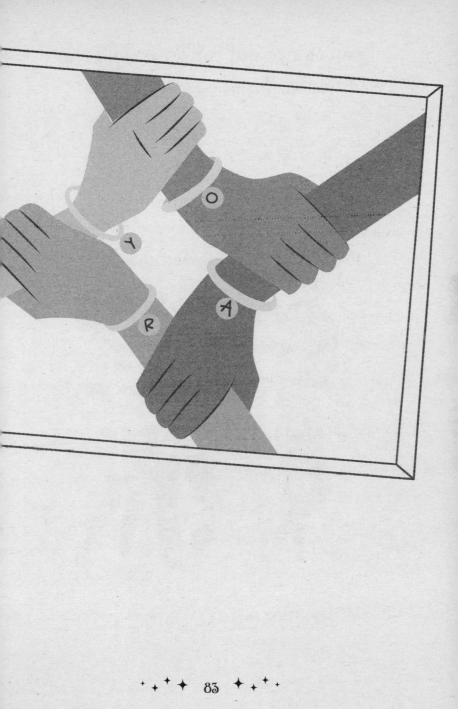

Keep an eye out for Rose Gold and
Friends: Yasmeen's Winter Fun:

Rose Gold
and Friends

Yasmeen's Winter Fun

ALICE HEMMING

Chapter 1

Waiting for ever

Yasmeen sat on a stool at the breakfast bar, bouncing her knee up and down rapidly. "Was that a car? I think I can hear someone outside!"

Her mum was busy unpacking groceries and sorting them into the kitchen cupboards. She stopped for a moment, holding a bunch of bananas in mid-air. "I'm sure they'll ring the buzzer when they get here. Just relax."

But Yasmeen couldn't. "Did you get all the food I asked for? Have we got tomato ketchup crisps? Oralie loves tomato ketchup flavoured crisps. And mini marshmallows? For hot chocolate?"

"I've got *everything* you put on the *very long* list," said Yasmeen's mum, holding out the scrap of paper. "Cakes, pizza, grapes, mini boxes of cereal… Nobody is going to go hungry this weekend." She paused. "But you must remember, Yasmeen, we're not expecting royalty. It's just your friends."

"Just my friends? *Just my friends*? You mean my *very best friends* in the *entire world*!"

Yasmeen had met the others – Amber, Rose and Oralie – at summer camp and they had become friends instantly. They had been planning this reunion ever since. For once, her mum wasn't working during the Christmas holidays and Yasmeen had been able to plan a few days of winter fun. But she was worried that this week would be a bit of a let-down after their action-packed days at camp. And what would the girls think of Yasmeen's little flat?

The intercom buzzed and Yasmeen nearly toppled off her bar stool. She slid along the wooden floor to answer it.

"Hi!" she shouted in excitement, before holding the receiver away from her ear because of the shrieking at the other end. It was Oralie, Amber and Rose. Amber's mum had given them all a lift. Yasmeen buzzed them in and raced to meet them at the door. "It's so good to see you!"

she cried, squeezing them all tightly in a group hug.

"I'M GETTING A PUPPY!" cried Oralie. "Sorry, I mean, hello and how are you and stuff like that, but I'm SO EXCITED about the puppy and it's all thanks to Rose letting us have Wriggly to stay in the summer—"

"This is all Oralie has talked about for the *entire* journey," said Amber with a smile.

"We put the radio on in the end but she talked over it," said Rose.

Yasmeen laughed. "I can't wait to hear all about it!" A big Old English Sheepdog padded over to greet the girls. She had a shaggy white and grey coat that covered her eyes.

"This is Mabel," said Yasmeen.

"Aww, hello," said Rose, putting out her hand for Mabel to sniff, which Mabel did before happily sitting down at Rose's feet.

"I think she likes you!" said Yasmeen.

Yasmeen led the girls through to a room with a wooden floor, which was lounge, dining room and kitchen all in one.

"You can put your stuff in my room but there isn't any room to sleep in there, so we'll be sleeping in here. In fact, we'll be doing everything in here."

"Wow! Your flat is so cool! I've never been in a flat before. I want a place *exactly* like this when I grow up," said Oralie. The room was decorated in black and white, with a fluffy grey rug in the middle. A breakfast bar separated the kitchen from the living space.

Amber looked around, open-mouthed. "You've got a huge TV! And bar stools!" The mums were sitting and chatting on them at that very moment.